Cover image courtesy of David and Jo Semple.

The Search for Santa!

Once upon a magical time, in the almost nearly now but a very long way away, a penguin called Pedro lived on a big white floe.

Now, I hear you ask, why would a penguin be called Pedro, a name which clearly would normally belong to someone from a country where Spanish was the language spoken?

Well, the answer is very simple.

On the edge of the Antarctic, where Pedro's family lived, there was a research station set up by the UNITED NATIONS, and one of the scientists who worked there was called Pedro and his job was to research penguins and so he fed them everyday from his little inflatable boat and told them stories about the lovely warm land that he came from.

He told them lots of other things too (I think that he must have been quite lonely). He told them how lucky they were not to be at the Arctic end of the world because at that end there were Polar Bears who thought penguins were very tasty.

But he also told them how UNLUCKY they were not to live at the Arctic end of the world because that was where Santa Claus lived and Santa Claus LOVED penguins and children and just about every living thing, except, of course, traffic wardens, for very obvious reasons. I mean, who would put a ticket on Santa's sleigh!

And so, one slightly warmer day than all of the others, when the eggs for the year began to crack and crumble to reveal the new chicks, one of the Mummy Penguins who had listened to all the lovely stories decided to call her new little boy chick, Pedro.

Pedro liked his name because it was different to all the other Penguin names that were fashionable at the time, which I would write about next except that there is no way to translate them into English so there's no point.

Pedro grew up to be a happy little chappy, who liked nothing more than sliding down the slippery slopes on the edge of the floe and splashing into the ice blue waters that washed around its base, where there were always plenty of fish to nibble on if he felt a bit peckish.

THEN, one terrible day, everything began to change!

The sky got bluer and the sun got warmer and the ice got slippier until the waves washed in and began to break up the great big floe into lots of little cubes and prisms and flat little splinters which, even though they were very pretty and sometimes made rainbows, were not great to live on if you were a penguin.

When the time had passed when it was meant to get all cold again and it just didn't, the Penguins huddled together for a chat (huddling made a chat possible because it stopped their bills shivering, so chattering became easier...)

The older Penguins decided that something had to be done! They had all heard the stories about

Santa Clause so they all agreed that the best thing to do would be for someone to go and find him and ask him for some help!

Pedro was huddled listening to this and thought that this was a very good idea and so he flapped his flipper to get the attention of the older penguins and said that he should be the one to go!

Everyone knew how bright he was, and how good he was at solving puzzles, so they all agreed!

A few sleeps later (they don't really have days and nights in the Antartic) Pedro set off.

He had worked out that bits of ice that broke off from Antartica could only go North, because they were at the South Pole, and so jumping on one and letting it carry him would be a very good start!

Everyone had turned out to see him off. All his classmates at Penguin Primary School had made banners and flags and their teacher had written a special poem, and here it is:

Pedro Penguin is a plucky little chap!
He's floating off North from the Southern ice cap.
Our ice is melting, but his will melt faster,
Let's hope he's not facing his own climate disaster!
When he finds Santa, all will end nice-ill-ly,

Which, in our little world means nice-ill-ly, ice-ill-ly!

All of the grown-ups applauded loudly!

That's. all of the grown-ups applauded loudly!!

Because they are very polite and they knew that if they didn't, the teacher would just read it again...

Then, with everyone waving and cheering, Pedro pushed off from the edge of the floe and bravely set off to go where no Penguin had gone before, or so he thought...

Two uncomfortable sleeps later Pedro was beginning to wonder if trying to find Santa had been such a good idea after all! The waves were ever so high, and the wind was ever so strong, and he could tell from where the sun was that he was going mostly sideways!

In fact, before he managed to stop a passing whale and get a tow, he had been around the world, twice! (It doesn't take very long to get around the world when you are near the top or the bottom).

Anyway, with the whales help he made it out of the Big Wavey Bit and soon found himself in the Lost Land of Patagonia!

He carefully parked his ice floe and went off in search of the South American Explorers Club, where he thought he might find a map and maybe even someone to help him.

And guess what! He did find a map and two helpers too.

One was a cuddly husky called Winter and the other was a cute snow leopard called Snuggle.

They were both looking to have an adventure and the three of them soon became firm friends and agreed to search for Santa together! Hooray!

First though they had to prepare!

They decided that travelling overland was the best idea now because the Americas go all the way from the Antarctic (almost) to the Arctic!

Pedro had made a handy flex-i-gloo from some random bamboo so they would always have somewhere to sleep, and the others knew lots of ways to get food so everything was going to be OK.

They knew that if they went uphill all the way, they couldn't get lost, and so they bravely set off!

They had lots of adventures and wrote them all down in little diaries that they kept with them.

We don't have time for all of them so here are some examples!

After sleep 61

Snuggle here! After we left Patagonia we followed the edge of the mountains. We went through a big desert beginning with "A" and past some very old stone buildings on hill tops. The locals told us that thousands of years ago the "Inca" used to live there.

Eventually we had to cross over the big mountains because they went all the way to the sea.

We were a bit stuck until we bumped into a big community of little furry creatures that knew they way! There were little with cute faces, and even though they were small, there were so many of them that they were able to pull and carry us over even the highest peaks until we found the narrow bit at the top end of South America, and there we said goodbye!

After sleep 96

Winter here! By now Pedro, Snuggle and I were the very best of friends! We had travelled all the way through Costa Rica, through California and Washington State and even British Columbia, and now we were in the biggest American state of them all, which was, of course, called ...Alaska!

Now we had to be super careful because there were VERY BIG BEARS ABOUT which, as we travelled further North, became more and more WHITE. These were the Polar Bears that we had been told about, so when we saw our first one, we knew that they must be near the ARCTIC CIRCLE.

Fortunately, the Big White Bear was a long way away and very busy with Bear business, so we were able to quietly creep by.

Some time later

Now, the Arctic Circle to some, is just an imaginary line on a map, but to magical adventurers in search of Santa, it is actually a physical barrier that they have to get through.

Luckily for our magical adventurers, there was a door.

Unluckily for our magical adventurers, it was locked.

Luckily for our magical adventurers, there was a keyhole to open the door.

Unluckily for our magical adventurers, they didn't have the key.

Luckily for Pedro, Winter and Snuggle, the key was in a key-safe next to the door which would only open for people who were on the nice list! Which, it turns out, they all were!

Once they had opened the door and gone through it and carefully closed it behind them and put the key back through a handy hole, they only had to hop, skip and jump a few hundred times and they found themselves at Santa's Secret City which sat glowing in the snow.

And here's a secret thing that most people don't know!

Most people think that the Northern Lights are caused by science stuff involving the sun, but they are actually caused by the glow from Santa's Secret City in the Snow, so now you know, but don't tell anybody else. SSSHHH!

Anyway, when Santa heard about the arrival of Pedro, Winter and Snuggle, he invited them to have lunch with him and Mrs Santa and they were soon deep in discussion about what they might be able to do to help the

Penguins at the South Pole and everybody else!

In the end Santa helped them make a plan, and this was it!

"I think', said Santa, "that it is very sad that lots of grown-ups (but not all, or even most, but certainly too many) care more about cars and home comforts than they do about keeping the planet safe for penguins and all the other living things that share the Earth.

So, what needs to be done will need to be done by the children and, of course, David Attenborough.

The children, and David Attenborough, will have to work together to:

MAKE THE CHANGE
THAT MATTERS IN
EVERYTHNG THEY
DO!

AND PUT THE
EARTH BEFORE
THEMSELVES SO THE
PLANET CAN PULL
THROUGH!

Then Santa told them that they should go to England to find some kind clever children to help them!

Santa knew how long they had been travelling so he arranged for them to use his magical network of inter-connected Igloos that would get them anywhere where there was another igloo in a tingily trice!

At this point in the story, Bernard and Eric and Zac, who had recently come back from England, put up their hands and said that they knew of a garden where an igloo was to be found AND where there were four young people and some nice, good-at-problem-solving grown-ups who would be happy to help!

"HOORAY!" said everyone.

But then Patch put up his hand. "I didn't want to say anything", he said, "but I think that the greedy grown-ups in charge have put padlocks on all the other igloos to stop Pedro and Winter and Snuggle from telling the children what to do! Padlocks with FOUR NUMBER COMBINATION LOCKS! And so, before the three friends can come out of the other end of the magical interconnecting network of igloos SOME CHILDREN are going to have to work out the numbers and unlock the padlock!"

Do you think that you can do that children!

Yes!

Hooray!

When you have the answers, you can go out into the garden and see if the magic igloo is there and if Pedro is waiting inside for Oscar and Winter is waiting inside for Summer and Snuggle is waiting inside for Sienna!

And here are the puzzles!!!!!!

Printed in Great Britain
by Amazon

34552508R00020